THIS BOOK
BELONGS TO:

This is a Parragon Publishing Book
This edition published in 2003
Parragon Publishing, Queen Street House, 4 Queen Street,
Bath, BA1 1HE, UK

Printed in China
ISBN 0 75257 688 7

Illustrations by:

Georgie Birkett, Stephanie Boey, Mario Capaldi,
Dorothy Clark, Kate Davies, Maggie Downer,
Frank Endersby, Serena Feneziani, Andrew Geeson,
Piers Harper, Elaine Keary, Angela Kincaid, Jane Molineaux, Claire
Mumford, Rikki O'Neill, Pauline Siewart,
Jessica Stockham and Linda Worrell.

Jacket illustration by Diana Catchpole

A collection of traditional rhymes, and original material written by Caroline Repchuk, Claire Keen and Andrew Charman

Contents

Girls and Boys

Girls and boys come out to play,
The moon doth shine as bright as day,
Leave your supper and leave your sleep,
And come with your playfellows into the street.
Come with a whoop, come with a call,
Come with a good will, or come not at all.
Up the ladder and down the wall,
A halfpenny bun will serve us all.
You find milk and I'll find flour,
And we'll have a pudding in half an hour.

Diddle, Diddle, Dumpling

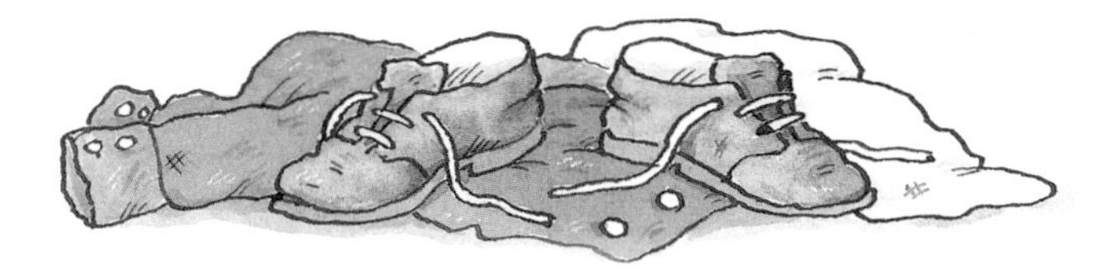

Diddle, diddle, dumpling, my son John,
Went to bed with his trousers on;
One shoe off, one shoe on,
Diddle, diddle, dumpling, my son John.

Pussy Cat, Pussy Cat

Pussy cat, pussy cat, where have you been?
I've been up to London to visit the Queen.
Pussy cat, pussy cat, what did you there?
I frightened a little mouse under her chair.

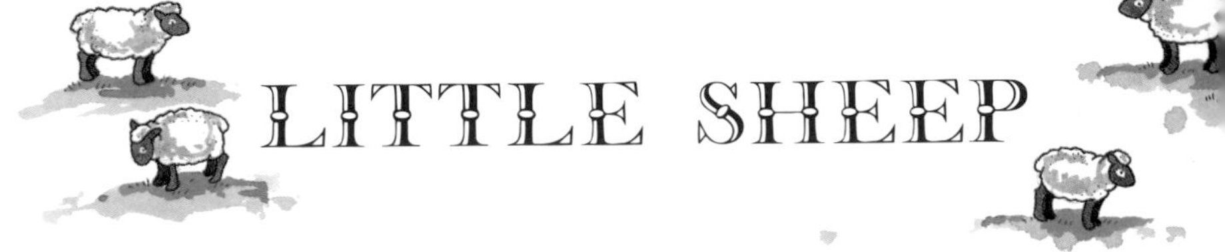

LITTLE SHEEP

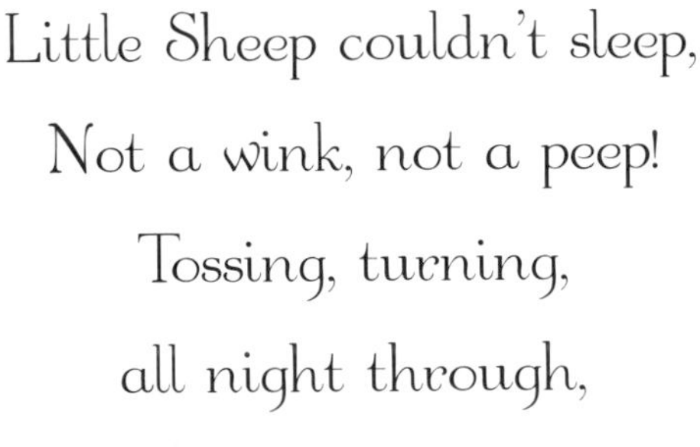

Little Sheep couldn't sleep,
Not a wink, not a peep!
Tossing, turning,
all night through,
What was poor Little Sheep to do?

Owl came by, old and wise,
Said, "Silly sheep, use your eyes –
You're lying in a field of sheep,
Try counting them to help you sleep!"

"Seven, four, thirteen, ten –
That's not right, I'll start again..."
Till daylight came, awake he lay
And vowed he'd learn to count next day!

MY BEST FRIEND

He cuddles me at bedtime,
And keeps me safe at night,
If I have a bad dream,
And wake up in a fright.

He is my constant playmate,
And often shares my tea,
He always lets me win at games,
And has a smile for me.

He shares in all my secrets,
And never shows surprise,
He listens to my problems,
With kindness in his eyes.

And when I'm feeling lonely,
On him I can depend,
He's more than just a teddy,
He is my best, best friend!

SOME TEDDY BEARS

Some teddy bears are tiny,
Some teddy bears are tall,
Some teddy bears are big and round,
And some teddy bears are small.

Some teddy bears are woolly,
Some teddy bears are rough,
Some teddy bears have shaggy fur,
And some are balls of fluff.

Some teddy bears look happy
Some teddy bears look sad,
Some teddy bears are very good,
And some teddy bears are bad.

But all teddy bears are loyal,
And all teddy bears are true,
And all teddy bears need lots of love
And hugs from me and you.

LITTLE DOG LOST

"Brrr," shivered Scruffy. "It's cold tonight, Mom. Why do we have to sleep outside in the cold when the cats are allowed to sleep in the house, in nice warm baskets?"

"We're farm dogs, dear," said Scruffy's Mom. "We have to be tough, and work hard to earn our keep. We don't have such a bad life," said Mom. "Now stop feeling sorry for yourself, and get some rest. We've got a lot of work to do tomorrow."

The next day, Scruffy woke early and went for a run through the grass, chasing rabbits, and sniffing at the flowers.

At the end of the lane he saw a big red truck parked outside a house. The back of the truck was open, and Scruffy thought he would just climb inside and take a look.

The truck was full of furniture including a big armchair with soft cushions. Scruffy clambered onto it. "I could doze all day, like a cat!" he told himself. He closed his eyes and fell fast asleep.

Scruffy was woken by a sharp jolt.

"Oh, no!" he groaned. "I must hurry back."

Then he saw that the truck doors were closed! He could hear voices outside.

"Oh, dear, I shall be in trouble," thought Scruffy, and he hid behind the chair.

The back of the truck opened and two men started unloading the furniture.

When Scruffy managed to creep out of the truck he found that he was in a big noisy town, full of buildings and cars.

Poor Scruffy was lost and very frightened.

All day long, Scruffy tried to find his way home. At last, he lay down feeling cold, and hungry. He began to howl miserably.

"What's the matter, pup?" he heard a man's kind voice say. "You look lost. Come home with me." Scruffy gave the man's hand a grateful lick, then jumped up and followed him home.

When they arrived at the man's house Scruffy sat on the doorstep, but the man said, "Come on in, you can't stay out there."

Scruffy went in and found a little poodle waiting to meet him. Scruffy stared at her, amazed. What had happened to her fur?

"You'd better take a bath before supper," said the man, looking at Scruffy's dirty white coat. The man washed him in a big tub, then brushed his tangled coat. Scruffy howled miserably. What had he done to deserve such punishment?

"Don't you like it?" asked the poodle, shyly.

"No, I don't," said Scruffy. "All this washing and cleaning is for cats!"

Then they had supper – small bowls of dry pellets. Scruffy sniffed in disgust. He was used to chunks of meat and a nice big bone.

"This looks like cat food," said Scruffy, miserably.

After supper the two dogs climbed into a big basket in the kitchen. Poor Scruffy tried to sleep but he was hot and uncomfortable. He missed counting the stars to help him fall asleep, and most of all he missed his mom.

"I want to go home," he cried, and big tears slipped down his nose.

The next day Scruffy was put on a lead. He hated being dragged along, without being able to sniff at things.

Then Scruffy saw his mom's head hanging through the window of the farmer's truck! He dragged the man over to where the truck was parked, and leapt up at the truck barking excitedly. The farmer had never seen Scruffy so clean! The man explained how he had found Scruffy and the farmer thanked him for taking such good care of him.

"I thought you had run away because you didn't like being a farm dog," she said gently.

"Oh, no, Mom," said Scruffy, quickly. "I love being a farm dog. I can't wait to get home to a nice big juicy bone and our little bed beneath the stars!"

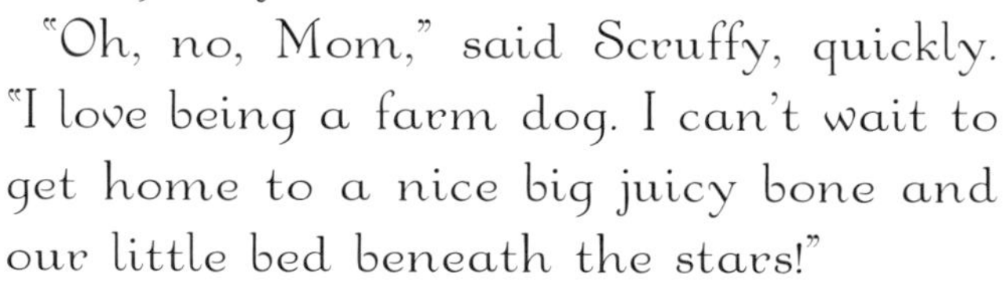

GREEDY BEAR

If there is one thing in the whole world that a teddy bear likes it is buns – big sticky buns with sugary tops and squishy middles. A teddy bear will do almost anything for a bun. But for one greedy little teddy bear called Clarence, sticky buns were to be his unsticking!

Rag Doll baked every kind of the most wonderful buns you could think of in the toy kitchen. Clarence loved them more than anyone else in the playroom.

"Please will you give me your bun - I'll polish your boots!" he would say to Tin Soldier.

If Tin Soldier wasn't too hungry, he'd agree. Some of the other toys would give Clarence their bun in return for a favor, and sometimes Clarence would eat five or six buns in one day!

Then he'd be busy washing the dolls' dresses, or cleaning the toy policeman's car. He would even stand still and let the clown throw custard pies at him!

You see, Clarence was not a lazy bear, but he was a greedy bear, and he was becoming a rather plump little greedy bear. All those buns were showing around his middle, and his fur was beginning to strain at the seams!

One day Clarence appeared in the playroom full of excitement. His owner, Penny, had told him that next week she was taking him on a teddy bears' picnic.

"There'll be honey sandwiches, ice-cream

and cookies – and lots and lots of buns!" Clarence told the others, rubbing his tummy. "I cant wait! All this excitement has made me rather hungry, I shall have a bun." He took a big sticky bun from under a cushion where he'd hidden it earlier.

"Oh, Clarence!" said Rabbit. "One of these days you will simply go pop!"

"Just be happy I don't like carrots!" said Clarence with a smile.

All that week Clarence was even busier. Every time he thought about the picnic it made him hungry, and then he'd have to find a bun. He would not listen when Rag Doll told him that his back seam was starting to come undone.

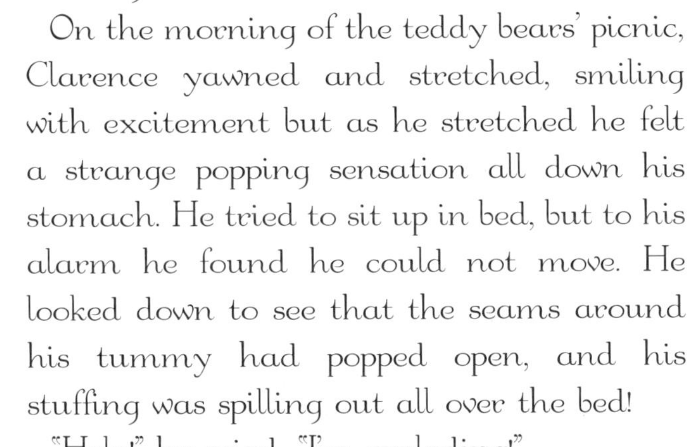

On the morning of the teddy bears' picnic, Clarence yawned and stretched, smiling with excitement but as he stretched he felt a strange popping sensation all down his stomach. He tried to sit up in bed, but to his alarm he found he could not move. He looked down to see that the seams around his tummy had popped open, and his stuffing was spilling out all over the bed!

"Help!" he cried. "I'm exploding!"

Just then, Penny woke up. "Oh, Clarence!" she cried when she saw him. "I can't take you to the teddy bears' picnic like that!"

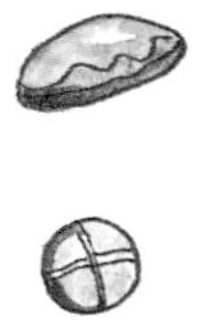

Penny's mommy sent Clarence to the toy hospital for a week.

When Clarence came back he was as good as new. Some of his stuffing had been taken out, and he was all sewn up again.

In the hospital he had lots of time to think about what a silly greedy bear he had been. How he wished he had not missed the picnic. The other teddies said it was the best day out they had ever had.

Penny had taken Rabbit. "It was terrible," moaned Rabbit. "Not a carrot in sight. But I saved you this bun."

"No thank you, Rabbit," said Clarence. "Funnily enough, I've gone off buns!"

Of course, Clarence did not stop eating buns for long, but from then on he stuck to one a day. And he still did favors for the others, only now he did them for free!

NIPPY SNIPPY

Eeeny, meeny, miney, mo,
Here comes Crab to
pinch your toe!
Shout out loud and
he'll let go -
Eeeny, meeny, miney, mo!

Nippy, snippy, snappy, snip,
Be careful when you
take a dip,
Or Crab will catch you
in his grip!
Nippy, snippy, snappy, snip!

The Muffin Man

Have you seen the muffin man,
The muffin man, the muffin man?
Have you seen the muffin man,
He lives in Drury Lane?

Oh yes, I've seen the muffin man,
The muffin man, the muffin man.
Oh yes, I've seen the muffin man,
He lives in Drury Lane.

Old King Cole

Old King Cole was a merry old soul,
And a merry old soul was he;
He called for his pipe,
And he called for his bowl,
And he called for his fiddlers three.

Little Miss Muffet

Little Miss Muffet
Sat on a tuffet,
Eating her curds and whey;
There came a big spider,
Who sat down beside her,
And frightened Miss Muffet away

Wee Willie Winkie

Wee Willie Winkie runs through the town,
Upstairs and downstairs in his nightgown,
Rapping at the windows,
crying through the locks,
"Are the children in their beds,
It's past eight o'clock?"

ACHOO!

Mouse's eyes filled up with water,
His little nose started to twitch,
A tingling tickled his whiskers,
And then his knees started to itch.
He got a bad case of the hiccups,
Then threw back his head in a sneeze,
And he said, "I'm most awfully sorry,
It's just I'm allergic to cheese!"

TEDDY BEAR'S PICNIC

Little Bear brought chocolate cake,
Raggy Bear brought honey,
Baby Bear brought ice-cream,
With butterscotch all runny!

Tough Old Ted brought cinnamon buns,
Silky Bear brought jello,
Shaggy Bear brought cookies and
Egg sandwiches all yellow!

Woolly Bear brought pecan pie,
Tiny Ted brought candy,
Mrs Bear brought little plates,
She thought would come in handy.

Off they set into the woods,
A sunny spot they found,
And had a teddies picnic,
As they shared the goodies round!

THE COW WHO JUMPED OVER THE MOON

Bouncy Bunny bounded across the field.

"I can bounce high in the air, watch me!" she called to the other animals on the farm. Her fluffy white tail bobbed up and down.

"Very good!" said Silly Sheep, who was easily impressed.

"Yes, very good," said Swift, the sheepdog. "But I can jump right over the gate," and

with that, he leapt straight over the gate.

"Amazing!" said Silly Sheep.

"Yes, amazing," said Harry Horse. "But I can jump right over that hedge. Watch me!" With that, he galloped up to the tall hedge and sailed straight over it.

"Unbelievable!" said Silly Sheep.

"Yes, unbelievable," said Daisy, the cow, chewing lazily on a clump of grass. "But not as unbelievable as me. I can jump right over the moon!"

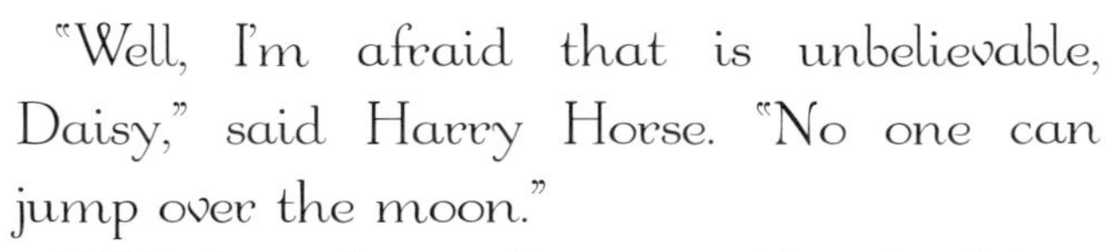

"Well, I'm afraid that is unbelievable, Daisy," said Harry Horse. "No one can jump over the moon."

"Well, I can," said Daisy, stubbornly. "And I can prove it! Watch me do it if you like!"

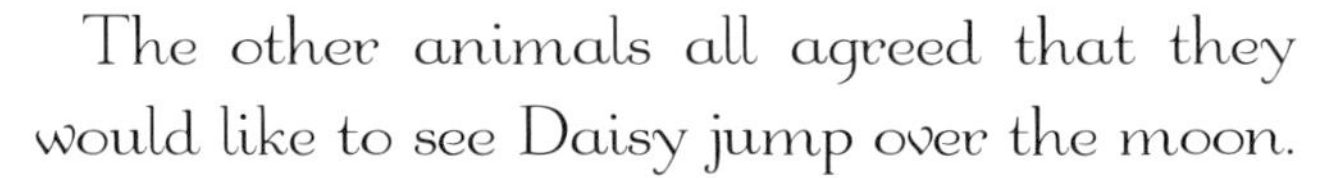

The other animals all agreed that they would like to see Daisy jump over the moon.

"Meet me here in the field tonight, then," Daisy said to them, "when the moon is full, and the stars are shining bright."

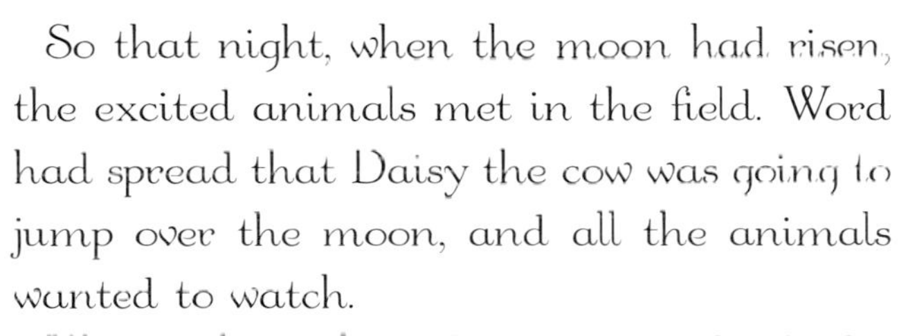

So that night, when the moon had risen, the excited animals met in the field. Word had spread that Daisy the cow was going to jump over the moon, and all the animals wanted to watch.

"Come along then, Daisy," said Swift, the sheepdog, as they waited impatiently. "Are you going to show us how you can jump over the moon, or not?"

The animals laughed, they thought that Daisy was just boasting, and that she would not really be able to do it.

"Yes, I am going to show you," said Daisy, "but first of all, you will have to come with me. This isn't the right spot." Daisy led the animals across the field, to the far side, where a little stream ran along the edge of the field, separating it from the dark woods on the other side.

"Now, stand back everyone, and give me some room," said Daisy. The animals did as they were asked, and watched Daisy with anticipation, giggling nervously. Whatever was she going to do?

Daisy trotted slowly back to the middle of the field, then ran towards the stream at great speed.

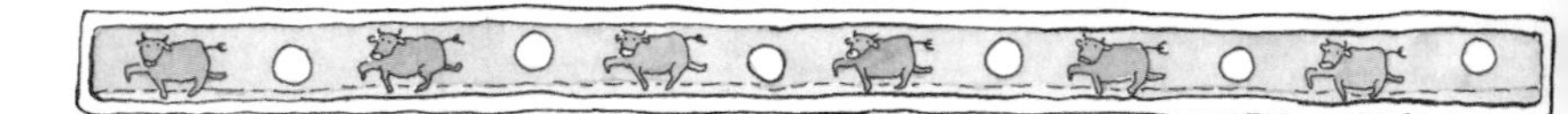

At the last moment, she sprang into the air, and sailed across the stream, landing safely on the other side.

"I did it!" cried Daisy. "Aren't you going to clap, then?" The other animals looked at each other in confusion.

"But you only jumped over the stream!" said Harry Horse, puzzled.

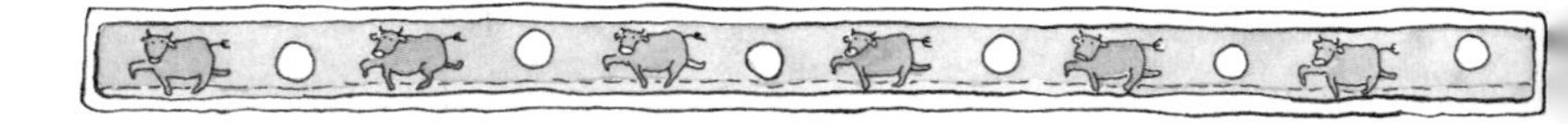

"Come here and take a closer look," called Daisy. When the animals looked down, reflected in the water shimmered the great full moon! The animals laughed when they realised Daisy had tricked them, and they clapped and cheered.

"That was a very good trick!" said Swift.

"Amazing!" said Silly Sheep. "Could someone explain it to me again, please?"

TOUGH TED LOSES HIS GROWL

Katie jumped out of bed, bursting with energy. Tough Ted opened one sleepy eye and stretched.

"Another morning," he yawned. "I don't suppose it will be a good one."

Tough Ted was a very old bear. He had belonged to Katie's mom when she was young. He had been a smart teddy then, and happy, but now he was in a sorry state and was always grumpy. He was the oldest of the toys and he had been through some tough times. The other toys loved him, but they were fed up with his constant moaning and groaning.

"When is this bed going to be made? I can't get comfortable with all these covers thrown back!" he complained. "Pull that blind down, the sun's shining straight into my eyes," he grumbled.

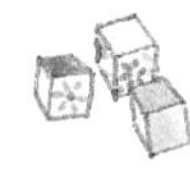

"If he doesn't stop complaining soon I'm going to stuff my hat in his mouth," whispered Soldier to Clown, as they sat on the shelf.

"Not if I put my juggling balls in there first!" said Clown. All the toys giggled.

"It's about time we taught him a lesson," said Rag Doll. "How do we stop him moaning?"

"What about sticking a band-aid over his mouth while he's asleep?" twittered Owl, who was always wise.

"That's a brilliant idea, Owl!" said Rag Doll, and everyone agreed.

So that night, Rag Doll fetched a band-aid from the bathroom cabinet, and stuck it over Tough Ted's mouth while he was asleep. Peace and quiet at last!

The next morning the alarm went off and Katie went into the bathroom. Tough Ted opened his eye and was just about to moan that the alarm was ringing, when he realized he could not open his mouth!

He pulled and stretched and twisted his face as hard as he could, but he could not get his mouth to open. When he looked and saw the band-aid in the mirror he was furious! He ripped it off and turned to face the other toys angrily.

"Who did this?" he bellowed. "When I find out who it was, there'll be trouble, growwwll! Have you no respect for an old bear?" He went on and on and on. He grew red in the face, and looked terribly cross. All the toys became quite scared.

Then, a funny thing happened. His voice began to crack. He tried to clear his throat, but he had lost his voice completely!

"Well it serves you right!" said Rag Doll. "All you do is moan, moan, moan. We put the band-aid on your mouth to teach you a lesson. But now you've moaned so much that you've made yourself lose your voice completely."

With that a big tear rolled down Tough Ted's cheek. He had not realized that he moaned so much, and he felt very sorry.

Rag Doll did not like seeing Tough Ted so sad. All the toys felt a bit guilty.

"I'll go and get you some honey from the kitchen," said Rag Doll. "It will soothe your throat. But you must promise not to start moaning again."

After Rag Doll had given Tough Ted a big spoonful of honey, he whispered, "I'm sorry. I promise I'll try not to moan any more. I didn't realize I'd become such a grumpy old bear."

Then all the toys gave Tough Ted a hug and Rag Doll gave him some more honey.

Tough Ted has tried very hard not to moan. But if he does, he thinks about the band-aid and quickly stops himself! And the rest of the toys do their best to look after him and keep him happy.

Turn Around

Turn around and touch the ground,
Turn around and touch the ground,
Turn around and touch the ground,
And fall right down.

Head, Shoulders, Knees and Toes

Head, shoulders, knees

and toes, knees and toes,

Head, shoulders, knees

and toes, knees and toes.

And eyes and ears

and mouth and nose.

Head, shoulders, knees

and toes, knees and toes.

The Baby in the Cradle

The baby in the cradle
Goes rock-a-rock-a-rock.

The clock on the dresser
Goes tick-a-tick-a-tock.

The rain on the window
Goes tap-a-tap-a-tap,

But here comes the sun,
So we clap-a-clap-a-clap!

I Am A Music Man

LEADER: I am a music man,
I come from far away,
And I can play.

ALL: What can you play?

LEADER: I play piano.

ALL: Pia, pia, piano, piano, piano,
Pia, pia, piano, pia, piano.

LEADER: I am a music man,
I come from far away,
And I can play.

ALL: What can you play?

LEADER: I play the big drum.

ALL: Boomdi, boomdi, boomdi boom,
Boomdi boom, boomdi boom,
Boomdi, boomdi, boomdi boom,
Boomdi, boomdi
boom.
Pia, pia, piano, piano,
piano
Pia, pia, piano, pia, piano.

LEADER: I am a music man,
I come from far away,
And I can play.

ALL: What can you play?

LEADER: I play the trumpet.

ALL: Tooti, tooti, tooti, toot,
Tooti, toot, tooti, toot,
Tooti, tooti, tooti, toot,
Tooti, tooti, toot.
Boomdi, boomdi, boomdi boom,
Boomdi boom, boomdi boom,
Boomdi, boomdi, boomdi boom,
Boomdi, boomdi boom.
Pia, pia, piano, piano, piano,
Pia, pia, piano, pia, piano.

Lucy Locket

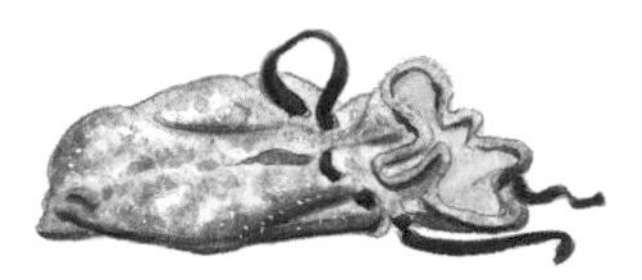

Lucy Locket lost her pocket,
Kitty Fisher found it.
Not a penny was there in it,
Only ribbon round it.

Aladdin's lamp is getting damp,
And is no longer gleaming.
It doesn't spark within the dark,
But you can't stop it steaming.

Cinderella's umbrella's
Full of holes all over.
Every time it starts to rain
She has to run for cover.

Polly Put The Kettle On

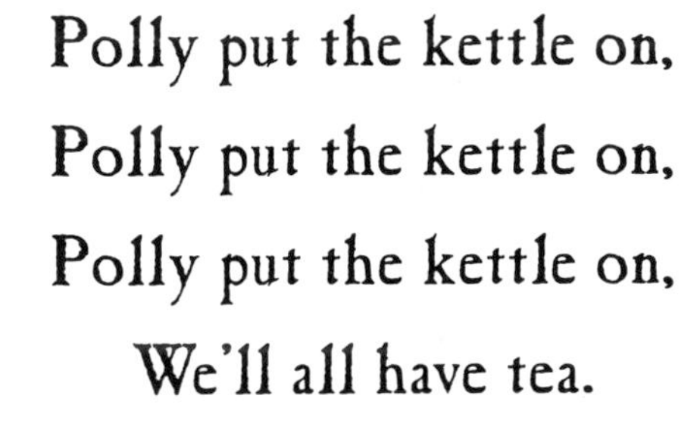

Polly put the kettle on,
Polly put the kettle on,
Polly put the kettle on,
We'll all have tea.

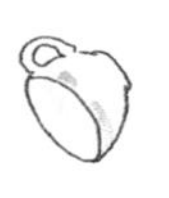

Sukey take it off again,
Sukey take it off again,
Sukey take it off again,
They've all gone away.

Jack and Jill

Jack and Jill went up the hill
To fetch a pail of water;
Jack fell down and broke
his crown
And Jill came tumbling after.

Up Jack got and home did trot
As fast as he could caper;
He went to bed to mend
his head
With vinegar and brown paper.

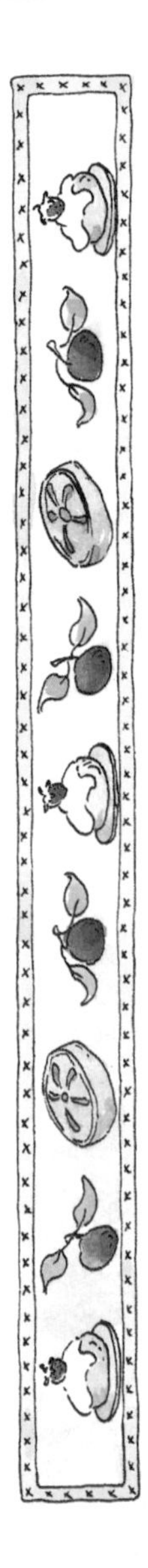

Georgie Porgie

Georgie Porgie, pudding and pie,
Kissed the girls and made them cry;
When the boys came out to play,
Georgie Porgie ran away.

Three Blind Mice

Three blind mice, three blind mice
See how they run, see how they run!
They all ran after the farmer's wife,
Who cut off their tails with a carving knife,
Did you ever see such a thing in your life,
As three blind mice?!

WHALE SONG

"Oh, what a beautiful morning!" sang Flippy, the whale, as streaks of sunlight filtered down through the clear blue ocean. He swam to and fro, twirled around, then whooshed through the waves, and jumped clear of the water in a perfect pirouette.

Flippy loved to sing and dance. He was a very graceful dancer but his singing was terrible. He boomed out song after song, and none of them were in tune! The dreadful sound echoed through the ocean for miles, sending all the ocean creatures diving for cover, as the waters shook around them. On sunny days the warm sun made Flippy want to sing and dance. It had got so bad that the other creatures had begun to pray for dull skies and rain.

"Something has to be done!" complained Wobble, the jellyfish. "His voice makes me shake so much that I can't see!"

"Well, I'm going as far away as possible." said Snappy, the lobster. "My head is splitting from Flippy's awful wailing."

"Someone will have to tell Flippy not to sing anymore," said Sparky, the stingray.

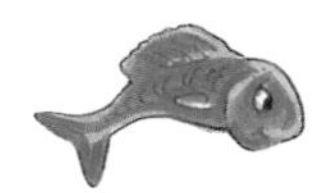

"It will hurt his feelings," said Wobble.

"Not as much as his singing hurts my ears!" snapped Snappy.

And so they decided that Sparky would tell Flippy the next day that they did not want him to sing any more songs. Wobble was right. Flippy was very upset when he heard that the others did not like his singing. He cried big, salty tears.

"I was only trying to enjoy myself!" he sobbed. "I didn't want to upset everyone."

"There, there," said Sparky, wishing he had not had to give the whale the bad news. "You can still enjoy dancing."

"It's not the same without music," said Flippy, miserably. "You can't get the rhythm." And he swam off into the deep waters, saying he wanted to be alone for a while.

As Flippy lay on the ocean floor, feeling very sorry for himself, a beautiful sound came floating through the water. It sounded like someone singing. Flippy wanted to know who was making such a lovely sound, so with a flick of his big tail, he set off to find out.

Peering out from behind a big rock, he saw that the voice belonged to a little octopus, who was shuffling and swaying about on the ocean floor. His legs were going in all directions, he tried to spin

around, but his legs got tangled and he crashed to the ground in a heap.

"Oh, dear," said Leggy, the octopus. "I seem to have eight left feet!"

"What are you trying to do?" Flippy asked, shyly.

"I was trying to dance," replied the octopus, blushing pink, "only I'm not very good at it."

"Well, I could teach you," said Flippy. "I'm a very good dancer – and there is something that I would love you to teach me..."

A few weeks later, Wobble, Snappy and Sparky were discussing how they missed having Flippy around, when they heard a beautiful sound floating towards them.

There were two voices singing in harmony!

"Surely that can't be Flippy!" said the others in surprise. But to their amazement, as the voices came closer they saw that, sure enough, it was Flippy, spinning and twirling as he danced gracefully towards them with his new friend!

THE NAUGHTY BEARS

One summer's day, Ben and Fraser's parents told them they were going to the beach.

"Yippee!" said Ben. "Can we take our teddies?"

"As long as you keep an eye on them," said Daddy. "We won't spend all afternoon looking for them if you lose them again!"

Ben and Fraser took their teddies everywhere, but they always lost them, and then there was a great hunt to find them. But the truth was, that when no one was looking, the naughty little teddies would run away in search of excitement and adventure.

Today was no different. When they arrived at the beach they unpacked their things and Mommy and Daddy sat reading. Soon Ben and Fraser were busy building sandcastles. When the naughty teddies saw that no one was looking, they jumped up and ran away giggling, all along the beach.

"Let's go exploring," said Billy. "I can see a cave over there." He pointed to a dark hole in the rocks close to the water.

"It looks a bit dark and scary," said Bella.

"Don't be silly," said Billy. "You're a bear. Bears like dark caves!"

The little bears clambered over the rocks and into the cave. In the dark Bella spotted something gleaming on the floor. She picked it up and showed it to Billy.

"Gold!" said Billy, "this must be a smuggler's cave! The smugglers might be here. Let's look!"

"No!" said Bella. "Let's go back." She turned and ran back outside, but her horror she saw the tide had come in, and cut the rocks off from the beach.

"Billy!" she called. "We're stranded!"

Meanwhile, Ben and Fraser had finished making sandcastles and found that their teddy bears were missing.

"Oh, no," groaned Daddy. "Not again!"

The family hunted all along the beach,

but there was no sign of the bears to be found. "Maybe they've been washed out to sea," said Fraser, his voice trembling at the thought.

Back at the cave the naughty teddies jumped up and down and waved their paws. "It's no use," said Bella, "they can't see us. We're too small."

"Don't worry," said Billy, trying to sound braver than he felt.

Just then, two men appeared from the other side of the rocks. The teddies froze – these must be the smugglers! They trembled in fear as the men picked them up, clambered over the rocks, and tossed them into a little boat that had been hidden from view. The teddies clung together at the bottom of the boat as the men jumped in and began to row. Where were they taking them?

After a while, the boat stopped and one of the men jumped out. Grabbing the bears he held them in the air high above his head, calling out, "Has anyone lost these bears?"

Everyone looked up, and Ben and Fraser raced over and grabbed their bears.

"Thank you," said Daddy. "We've been looking everywhere for them."

"We found them up by that cave," said one of the men, pointing over to the cave. "Your kids must have left them there."

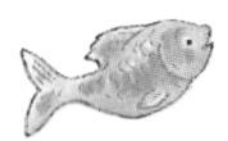

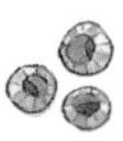

"But they've been here building sandcastles all afternoon..." said Daddy, looking puzzled.

No one ever did find out how the naughty teddies got to the cave, or where the little coin in Billy's pocket came from. But from then on Daddy said they had to stay at home. The naughty teddies didn't really mind. They'd had enough adventures for the time being. And it gave them lots of time to play their favorite game – hide and seek!

Round and Round the Garden

Round and round
the garden,
Like a teddy bear;

One step, two steps,
Tickle you under there.

Round and round
the haystack,
Went the little mouse.

One step, two steps,
In this little house.

If You're Happy and You Know It

If you're happy and you know it,
Clap your hands.
If you're happy and you know it,
Clap your hands.
If you're happy and you know it,
And you really want to show it,
If you're happy and you know it,
Clap your hands.

If you're happy and you know it,

Nod your head, etc.

If you're happy and you know it,

Stamp your feet, etc.

If you're happy and you know it,

Say "ha, ha!", etc.

If you're happy and you know it,

Do all four!

ELEPHANTS NEVER FORGET

I woke up this morning, astounded,
To find my long trunk in a knot!
I know it must be to remind me
To remember something I've forgot!

But though I've been thinking all morning
I haven't remembered it yet.
Still I'm sure I will think of it soon,
Because elephants never forget!

Simple Simon

Simple Simon met a pieman
Going to the fair,
Says Simple Simon to the pieman
"Let me taste your ware."
Says the pieman to Simple Simon,
"Show me first your penny."
Says Simple Simon to the pieman,
"Indeed I have not any."

Simple Simon went a-fishing
For to catch a whale;
But all the water he had got
Was in his mother's pail.

LAZY TEDDY

There was nothing Lazy Teddy liked more than to be tucked up in Joshua's bed. Every morning the alarm clock would ring and Joshua would leap out of bed and fling open the curtains. "I love mornings!" he'd say, as the sun poured in through the window. "You're crazy!" Teddy would mutter, and he'd burrow to the bottom of the bed, where he'd snooze happily for the rest of the morning.

"Come out and play, you lazy bear," Joshua would call. But Lazy Teddy wouldn't budge. He would just snore even louder.

Joshua wished that Teddy would be more lively, like his other friends' bears. He loved having adventures, but they would be even better if Teddy would share them with him.

One evening, Joshua decided to have a talk with Teddy. He told him all about the fishing trip he'd been on that day with his friends and their teddy bears.

"It was lots of fun, Teddy. I wish you'd been there. It's time you stopped being a lazybones. Tomorrow is my birthday, and I'm having a party. There will be games, and presents and ice-cream. Please promise you'll come?"

"It does sound like fun," said Teddy. "Okay, I promise. I'll get up just this once."

The next morning, Joshua was up bright and early. "Yippee, it's my birthday today!" he yelled, and he pulled the covers off his bed. "Come on, Teddy, time to get up!"

"Just five more minutes!" groaned Teddy, and fell straight back to sleep. Joshua came back after breakfast and Teddy still wasn't up. Joshua felt quite cross with Teddy. He reached over and poked him in the tummy. Teddy opened one eye and growled. "Wake up, Teddy! You promised, remember?" said Joshua.

Teddy yawned. "Oh, if I must!" he said. He muttered and grumbled while he washed, brushed his teeth and put on his best red vest.

"There, I'm ready!" he said.

"Good," said Joshua. "About time too!"

Just then the doorbell rang, and Joshua ran to answer it. "I'll fetch you in a minute," he said to Teddy. But when he returned there was no sign of Teddy, just a gentle snoring coming from the bottom of the bed.

Joshua was so cross and upset with Lazy Teddy, that he decided to leave him right where he was. Deep down though, he was hurt that Teddy wouldn't keep his promise.

Joshua enjoyed his party, but he wished that Teddy had been there. That night when he got into bed, he lay crying quietly into his pillow.

Teddy lay awake in the dark, listening to Joshua crying. Teddy knew Joshua was crying because he had let him down, and he felt very ashamed of himself.

"I'm sorry!" whispered Lazy Teddy, and he snuggled up to Joshua and stroked him with a paw until he fell asleep.

The next morning, the alarm clock rang and Joshua leapt out of bed. But what was this? Teddy had leapt out of bed too! Joshua looked at him in amazement.

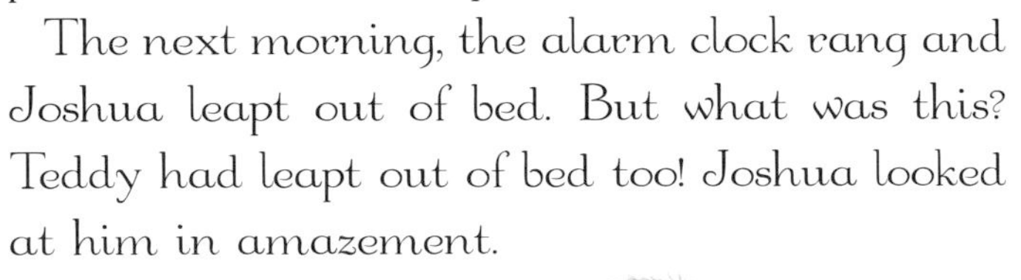

"What are we both doing today, Joshua?" asked Teddy.

"G...g...going for a picnic," stammered Joshua.

"Let's get ready then," said Teddy. And from then on, Teddy was up bright and early every day, ready to enjoy another day of adventures with Joshua, and he never let him down again.

Old Mother Hubbard

Old Mother Hubbard
Went to the cupboard
To fetch her poor dog a bone,
But when she got there
The cupboard was bare
And so the poor dog had none.

Tom, Tom, The Piper's Son

Tom, Tom, the piper's son,
Stole a pig and away he run!
The pig was eat, and Tom was beat,
And Tom went roaring down the street.

Knick Knack Paddy Whack

This old man, he played one,
He played knick knack on my drum.
With a knick knack paddy whack,
give a dog a bone,
This old man went rolling home.

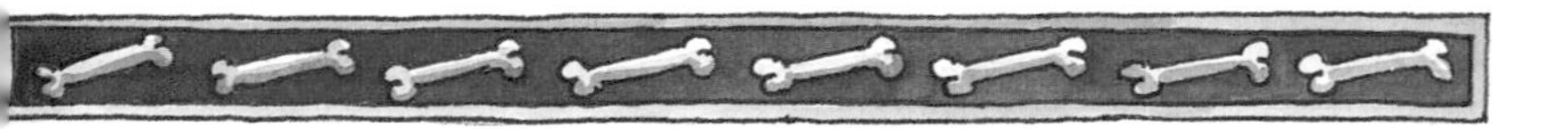

This old man, he played two,
He played knick knack on my shoe.
With a knick knack paddy whack,
give a dog a bone,
This old man went rolling home.

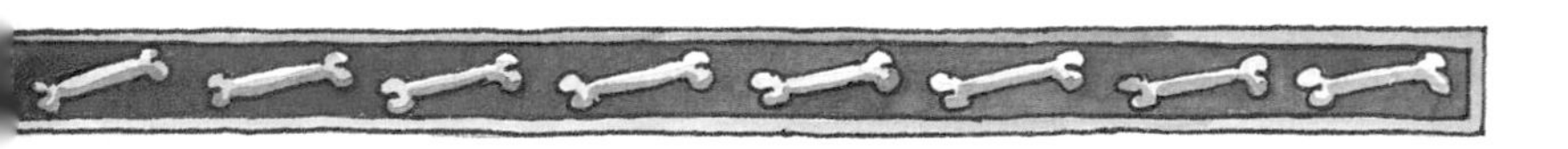

This old man, he played three,
He played knick knack on my knee.
With a knick knack paddy whack,
give a dog a bone,
This old man went rolling home.

This old man, he played four,
He played knick knack on my door.
With a knick knack paddy whack,
give a dog a bone,
This old man went rolling home.

This old man, he played five,
He played knick knack on my hive.
With a knick knack paddy whack,
give a dog a bone,
This old man went rolling home.

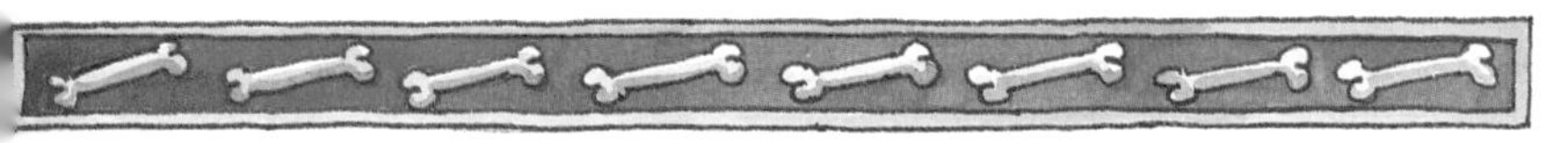

The Owl and the Pussy-cat

The Owl and the Pussy-cat went to sea
In a beautiful pea-green boat,
They took some honey, and plenty of money,
Wrapped up in a five-pound note.
The Owl looked up to the stars above,
And sang to a small guitar,
"O lovely Pussy! O Pussy, my love,
What a beautiful Pussy you are,
You are, you are!
What a beautiful Pussy you are!"

Pussy said to the Owl, "You elegant fowl!
How charmingly sweet you sing!
"O let us be married! Too long we have tarried:
But what shall we do for a ring?"
They sailed away, for a year and a day,
To the land where the Bong-tree grows,
And there in a wood a Piggy-wig stood,
With a ring at the end of his nose,

His nose, his nose,
With a ring at the end
of his nose.

"Dear Pig, are you willing to sell for one shilling
Your ring?" Said the Piggy, "I will."
So they took it away, and were married next day
By the Turkey who lives on the hill.
They dined on mince, and slices of quince,
Which they ate with a runcible spoon;
And hand in hand, on the edge of the sand,
They danced by the
light of the moon,
The moon, the moon,
They danced by the light of the moon.

TEDDY BEAR TEARS

"Boo hoo! I want to go home!"

Mavis the fairy flew by the garbage dump, holding her nose, and heard crying coming from the smelly pile of garbage.

"Those sound like teddy bear tears," she said to herself. "I must see if I can help."

There amongst a heap of potato peelings and banana skins sat a very old, sad teddy. Mavis held his paw, while he told her what had happened:

"My owner, Matylda, had to clean out her room. She's messy, but she's sweet and kind," Teddy sniffed. "She threw me out by mistake – she didn't realize I was tucked up having a sleep inside an old blanket.

Then some men in a big dirty truck emptied me out of the trashcan and brought me here. But I want to go home!" And with that poor Teddy started to cry again.

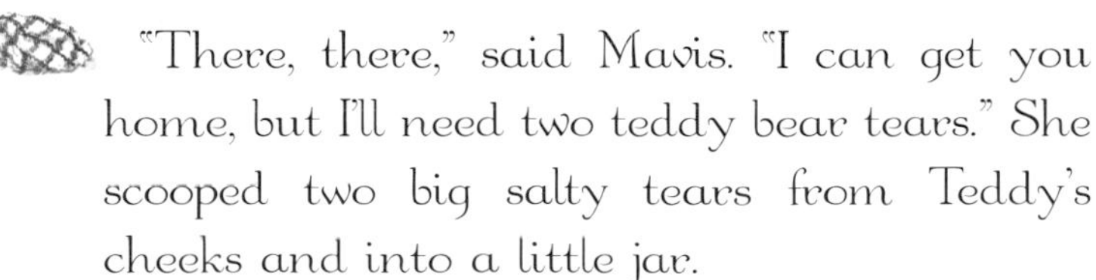

"There, there," said Mavis. "I can get you home, but I'll need two teddy bear tears." She scooped two big salty tears from Teddy's cheeks and into a little jar.

"What do you need those for?" asked Teddy, feeling rather bewildered.

"Just a little fairy magic!" said Mavis. And with a wave of her wand she disappeared.

Teddy pulled the blanket around him, and sat trying to be brave, and not to cry. He stayed like that all night, feeling cold and alone and frightened. How he wished he was back in his warm cozy home.

Meanwhile Mavis was very busy. She flew back and forth until she heard the sound of sobbing coming from an open window. She flew down onto the window sill and peered inside. A little girl was lying on the bed, with her mommy sitting beside her.

"I want my teddy!" she cried.

"Well if you weren't so messy Matylda, you wouldn't lose things," said Mommy gently.

"I cleaned my room today!" said Matylda.

"Well, try and go to sleep now," said Mommy, kissing her goodnight, "and we'll look for Teddy in the morning."

At last Matylda fell fast asleep. Then Mavis flew down and, opening the jar, rubbed Teddy's tears onto Matylda's eyes. The fairy magic began to work and Matylda started to dream. She could see an old tire, newspapers, a blanket... wait a minute, it was her blanket, and there, wrapped inside it was

her teddy, with tears running down his cheek! Teddy was at the garbage dump!

Matylda remembered her dream as soon as she woke up. She ran downstairs to Mommy, and told her all about it.

"We have to go to the garbage dump! We have to save Teddy!" said Matylda.

Mommy tried to explain that was all a dream, but Matylda wouldn't listen, so in the end they set off to take a look.

As they arrived a big machine was scooping up garbage and heading for the crusher. There, clinging to the scoop, was Teddy!

Mavis hovered in the air above him.

"Don't worry, we'll save you!" she said. Her wand made a bright flash above Teddy. Matylda looked up and spotted him at once.

"There he is!" she cried, pointing frantically at Teddy. "He's going to be squashed! Mommy, do something, quick!" Mommy ran up to the man driving the machine, waving her arms in the air.

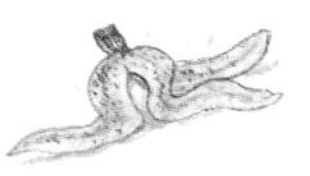

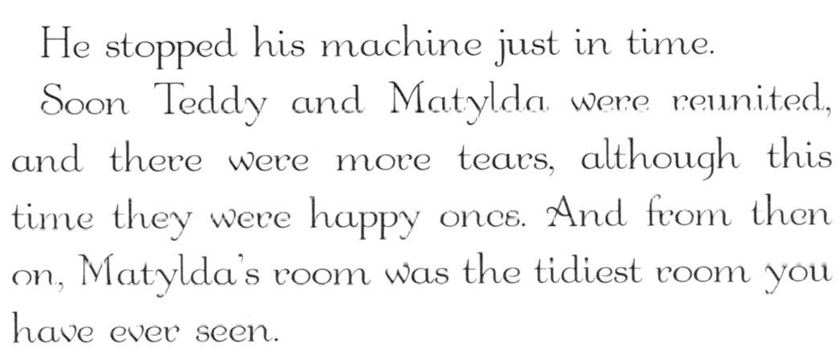

He stopped his machine just in time.

Soon Teddy and Matylda were reunited, and there were more tears, although this time they were happy ones. And from then on, Matylda's room was the tidiest room you have ever seen.

The Lion and the Unicorn

The Lion and the Unicorn
Were fighting for the crown;
The Lion beat the Unicorn
All around the town.

Some gave them white bread,
And some gave them brown;
Some gave them plum cake,
And drummed them
out of town.

Here's a Ball for Baby

Here's a ball for baby,
Big and fat and round.

Here is baby's hammer,
See how it can pound.

Here are baby's soldiers,
Standing in a row.

Here is baby's music,
Clapping, clapping so.

Here is baby's trumpet,
TOOTLE-TOOTLE-OO!

Here's the way the baby
Plays at peek-a-boo.

Here's a big umbrella,
To keep the baby dry.

Here is baby's cradle,
Rock-a-baby-bye.

Little Cottage in the Wood

Little cottage in the wood,
Little old man by the window stood,
Saw a rabbit running by,
Knocking at the door.
"Help me! Help me! Help me!" he said,
"Before the huntsman shoots me dead."
"Come little rabbit, come inside,
Safe with me abide."

A Frog He Would A-Wooing Go

A frog he would a-wooing go,
Heigh ho! says Rowley,
Whether his mother would let him or no,
With a rowley, powley, gammon and spinach,
Heigh ho! says Anthony Rowley.

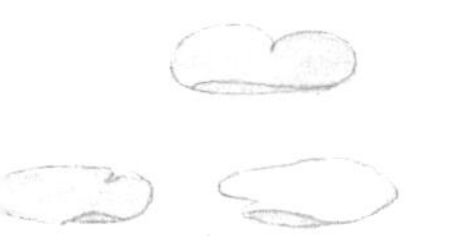

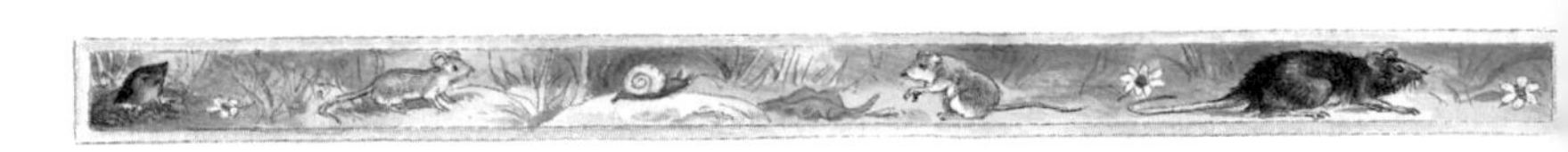

So off he set with his opera hat,
Heigh ho! says Rowley,
And on the way he met with a rat,
With a rowley, powley, gammon and spinach,
Heigh ho! says Anthony Rowley.

Pray, Mister Rat, will you go with me?
Heigh ho! says Rowley,
Kind Mistress Mousey for to see?
With a rowley, powley, gammon and spinach,
Heigh ho! says Anthony Rowley.

They came to the door of Mousey's hall,
Heigh ho! says Rowley,
They gave a loud knock and they
gave a loud call.
With a rowley, powley, gammon and spinach,
Heigh ho! says Anthony Rowley.

Pray, Mistress Mouse, will you
give us some beer?
Heigh ho! says Rowley,
For Froggy and I are fond of good cheer.
With a rowley, powley, gammon and spinach,
Heigh ho! says Anthony Rowley.

But while they were all a merry-making,
Heigh ho! says Rowley,
A cat and her kittens came tumbling in.
With a rowley, powley, gammon and spinach,
Heigh ho! says Anthony Rowley.

The cat she seized the rat by the crown,
Heigh ho! says Rowley,
The kittens they pulled the little
mouse down.
With a rowley, powley, gammon and spinach,
Heigh ho! says Anthony Rowley.

This put Mister Frog in a terrible fright.
Heigh ho! says Rowley,
He took up his hat and he wished
them goodnight.
With a rowley, powley, gammon and spinach,
Heigh ho! says Anthony Rowley.

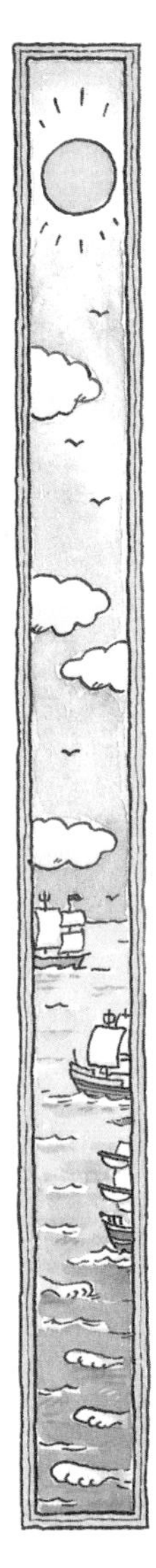

Bobby Shaftoe

Bobby Shaftoe's gone to sea,
Silver buckles at his knee,
He'll come back and marry me,
Bonny Bobby Shaftoe.

Little Jack Horner

Little Jack Horner,
Sat in a corner,
Eating a Christmas pie.
He put in his thumb,
And pulled out a plum,
And said, "What a good boy am I!"

Little Boy Blue

Little Boy Blue, come blow your horn
The sheep's in the meadow,
the cow's in the corn.
Where is the boy who looks after the sheep?
He's under the haystack fast asleep.
Will you wake him? No, not I!
For if I do, he's sure to cry.

Yankee Doodle

Yankee Doodle came to town,
Riding on a pony,
He stuck a feather in his cap
And called it macaroni.

POOR LITTLE TED

Poor little Ted
Fell out of bed,
And found that he had
A big bump on his head!

He let out a scream,
I woke from my dream,
And soon made him better
With cake and ice-cream!

IN A SPIN

I had a little teddy,
He went everywhere with me,
But now I've gone and lost him,
Oh, where can my teddy be?

I've looked behind the sofa,
I've looked beneath the bed,
I've looked out in the garden,
And in the garden shed!

I've looked inside the bathtub,
And underneath my chair,
Oh, where, oh, where is Teddy?
I've hunted everywhere!

At last I try the kitchen,
My face breaks in a grin.
There's Teddy in the washtub –
Mom's sent him for a spin!

BIRTHDAY BUNNIES

"It's my first birthday tomorrow!" announced Snowy, very proudly. "Isn't that exciting?"

"Yes, very exciting!" said Whiskers, her brother. "Because it's my birthday too!"

"And mine!" said Patch.

"And mine!" said Nibble.

"And mine!" said Twitch.

"Do you think mom and dad have got a surprise for us?" asked Snowy.

"I hope so!" said Whiskers.

"Me too!" said Patch.

"Me too!" said Nibble.

"Me too!" said Twitch.

Mrs Rabbit was listening as her children were getting ready for bed. She heard the little bunnies chattering excitedly about their birthdays the next day.

How could she make it a special day for them? She thought very hard, and later that evening, when Mr Rabbit came home, she said: "It is the childrens' first birthday tomorrow, and I'm making a surprise carrot cake for them. Could you go and dig some nice fresh carrots from your vegetable garden?"

"Certainly, dear," said Mr Rabbit, and off he went back outside.

Mr Rabbit was proud of the carrots he grew. They were crunchy, sweet and delicious, every year they won a prize at the Country Show. So you can imagine his dismay when he arrived at his vegetable patch to find that every single carrot had been dug up and stolen!

He marched home. "Someone has stolen my carrots!" he announced to his wife, crossly. "And I am going to find out just who it is!"

It was getting late, but he went outside, and set off to find the naughty person.

First of all he stopped at Hungry Hare's house, and knocked at the door.

"Someone has stolen my carrots!" Mr Rabbit said. "Do you know who?"

"Oh, yes," said Hungry Hare. "But it wasn't me." And Hungry Hare would say no more.

Next Mr Rabbit went to Sly Fox's house.

"Someone has stolen my carrots!" he said. "Do you know who?"

"Oh, yes," said Sly Fox. "But it wasn't me." Although Mr Rabbit begged him, Sly Fox would say no more.

Mr Rabbit went to Bill Badger's house, and asked if he knew who had taken the carrots.

"Yes, I do know," he said. "And it wasn't me."

And like the others, he would say no more. It was the same wherever Mr Rabbit went. He got very cross, and stamped his foot, no one would tell him who had stolen his carrots!

"You'll find out soon," said Red Squirrel.

So Mr Rabbit went home feeling very puzzled. "It seems that everyone knows who it was, but no one will tell me!" said Mr Rabbit to his wife.

"Well, I don't know who it was. All I know is that we have no surprise for the children's birthday." Feeling very confused, they went to bed.

Next day the little bunnies came running into the kitchen, where their parents were having breakfast.

"Happy birthday, everyone!" called Snowy.

"Happy birthday!" cried all the little bunnies.

"Now, it's not much, but I wanted to give each of you a surprise!" Snowy went on. "By the way, I hope you don't mind, Dad." And with that Snowy pulled out a box of juicy carrots, each tied with a bow, and handed one to each of her brothers and sisters.

"Snap!" cried Whiskers, "I had just the same idea!" and he pulled out another box of carrots.

"Me too!" said Patch.

"Me too!" said Nibble.

"Me too!" said Twitch.

"So that's what happened to my carrots!" cried Mr Rabbit, in amazement. "I thought they had been stolen!" And when he told the little bunnies the story they laughed till their sides ached. Then Mrs Rabbit put on her apron and shooed them outside.

"Just leave the carrots with me," she said. "I have a birthday surprise of my own!"

And so the mystery was solved. It turned out that Hungry Hare had seen the little bunnies creep out one by one, and each dig up a few carrots when they thought no one was looking. He knew it was their birthdays and he guessed what they were doing. He had told the other forest folk, and everyone thought it was a great joke.

Mr Rabbit felt ashamed that he had been so cross with everyone, when they were really just keeping the secret. To apologise, he invited them for a special birthday tea that afternoon, which the little bunnies thought was a great surprise.

And of course the highlight of the day was when Mrs Rabbit appeared from the kitchen carrying, what else, but an enormous carrot cake!

WOBBLY BEAR

Mr and Mrs Puppety owned an old-fashioned toy shop. They made toys by hand, but they were getting old and their eyesight was bad.

"It's time we got an apprentice toymaker," said Mr Puppety to his wife. They soon found a young lad called Tom to work for them. He spent his first week making a teddy bear. He showed the finished bear to Mr and Mrs Puppety.

"He looks very cuddly," said Mrs Puppety.

Tom was pleased that they liked his bear and he went off home whistling happily.

"He is a lovely bear," said Mr Puppety, "but his head is a bit wobbly."

"I know," said his wife, "but it's Tom's first try. Let's just put him up there on the shelf with the other teddy bears."

3
2
1

That night Wobbly Bear started to cry. He had heard what Mr and Mrs Puppety had said.

"What's wrong?" asked Brown Bear, who was sitting next to him.

"My head is on wobbly," sobbed Wobbly Bear.

"Does it hurt?" asked Brown Bear.

"No," replied Wobbly Bear.

"Then why are you crying?" asked Brown Bear.

"Because nobody will want to buy a wobbly bear. I'll be left in this shop forever and nobody will ever take me home and love me," he cried.

"Don't worry," said Brown Bear. "You look fine to me. Just try your best to look cute and cuddly and you'll soon have someone to love you." This made Wobbly Bear feel much happier and he soon fell fast asleep.

The next day the shop was busy, but nobody paid any attention to Wobbly Bear. Then a little boy looked up at the shelf and cried, "Oh, what a lovely bear. Can I have that one, Daddy?"

Bear's heart lifted as the little boy's daddy reached up to his shelf. But he picked up Brown Bear instead and handed him to the little boy. Wobbly Bear felt sadder than ever. Nobody wanted him. All of his new friends would get sold and leave the shop, but he would be left on the shelf gathering dust. Poor old Wobbly Bear!

Now, Mr and Mrs Puppety had a little granddaughter called Jessie who loved to visit the shop and play with the toys. All the toys loved her because she was gentle and kind. It so happened that the next time she came to visit it was her birthday, and her grandparents told her she could choose any toy she wanted as her present.

"She won't choose me," thought Wobbly Bear sadly. "Not with all these other beautiful toys."

But to Wobbly's amazement, Jessie pointed at his shelf and said, "I'd like that wobbly bear please. No one else will have a bear quite like him."

Mr Puppety smiled and gave Wobbly to Jessie. She hugged and kissed him, and Wobbly felt so happy he almost cried. She took him home and put a smart red bow around his neck ready for her birthday party. He felt very proud indeed.

Soon the other children arrived, each carrying their teddy bears under their arms.

Wobbly Bear could not believe his eyes when he saw the little boy with his friend Brown Bear!

"I'm having a teddy bears' picnic," Jessie explained to him, hugging him tight. All of the children and the bears had a wonderful time, especially Wobbly. He had found a lovely home, met his old friend and made lots of new ones.

"See, I told you not to worry," said Brown Bear.

"I know," said Wobbly. "And I never will again."

Scrub Your Dirty Face

Scrub your dirty face,
Scrub your dirty face,
With a rub-a-dub-dub,
And a rub-a-dub-dub,
Scrub your dirty face.

Clap Your Hands

Clap your hands, clap your hands,
Clap them just like me.
Touch your shoulders, touch your shoulders,  
Touch them just like me.
Tap your knees, tap your knees,
Tap them just like me.
Shake your head, shake your head,
Shake it just like me.
Clap your hands, clap your hands,
Then let them quiet be.

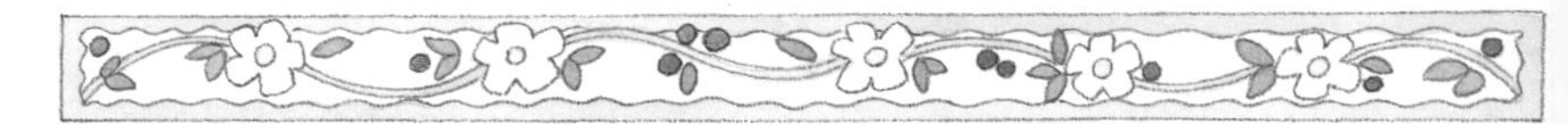

Dancing Round the Maypole

Dancing round the maypole,
Dancing all the day,
Dancing round the maypole,
On the first of May,
Dancing round the maypole,
What a merry bunch,
Dancing round the maypole,
Till it's time for lunch.

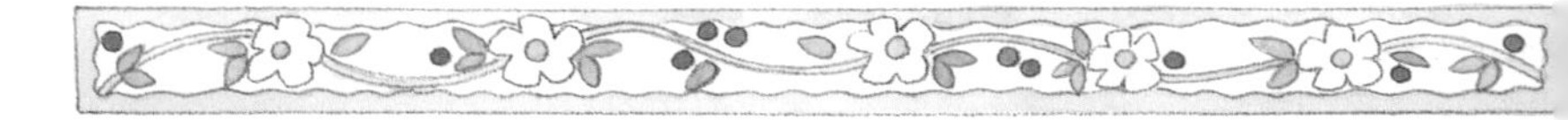

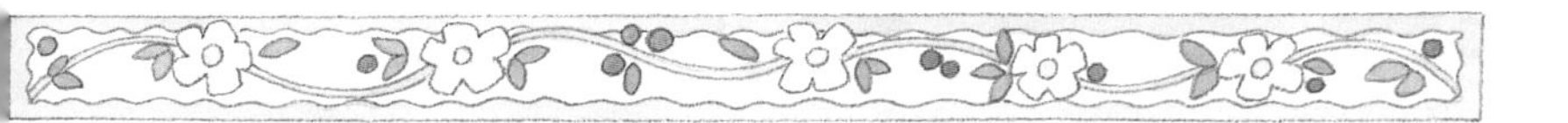

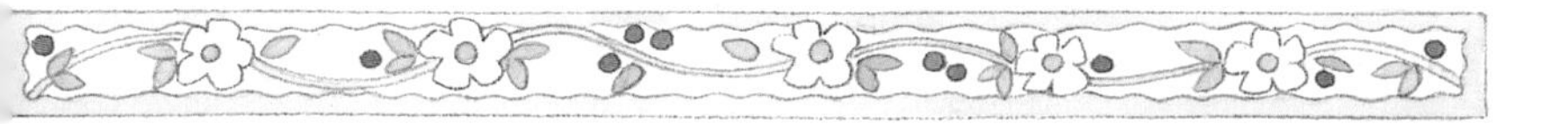

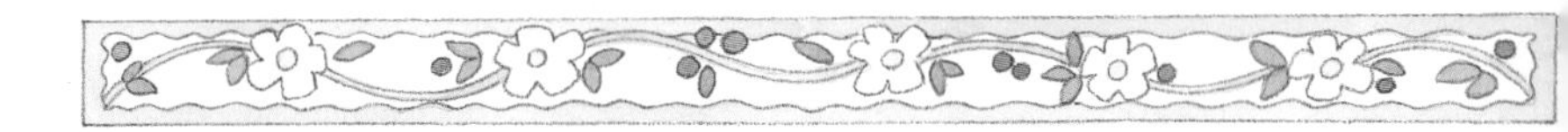

Dancing round the maypole,
Shouting out with glee,
Dancing round the maypole,
Till it's time for tea.
Dancing round the maypole,
Blue and white and red,
Dancing round the maypole,
Till it's time for bed.

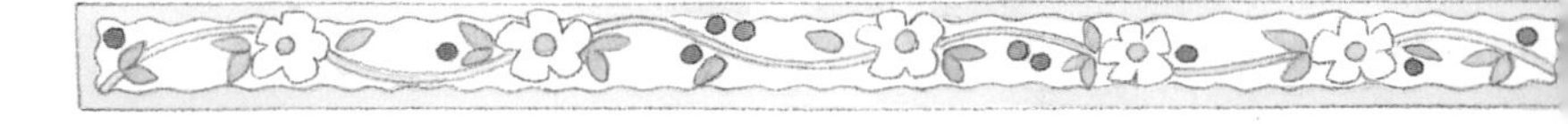

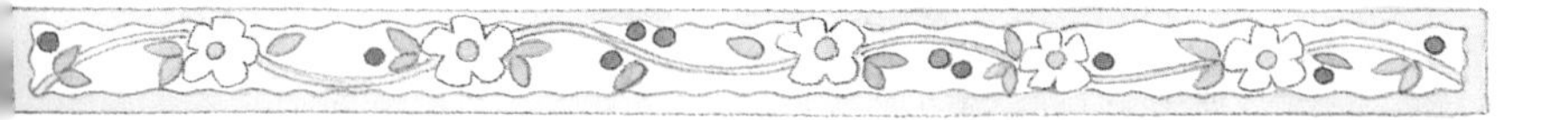

One, Two, Three, Four, Five

One, two, three, four, five,
Once I caught a fish alive.
Six, seven, eight, nine, ten,
Then I let him go again.
Why did you let him go?
Because he bit my finger so!
Which finger did he bite?
This little finger on the right.

Little Bo Peep

Little Bo Peep has lost her sheep
And doesn't know where to find them;
Leave them alone, and they'll come home
Bringing their tails behind them.

CAT'S CHORUS

We meet every night
On the same garden wall,
And if you're in luck
You may hear our call:
With a howl and a yowl,
and a hullaballoo,
We're the cat's chorus,
singing for you!

Fifi's soprano,
Butch sings the bass,
Kipper's a baritone,
Bert sets the pace.
Chorus

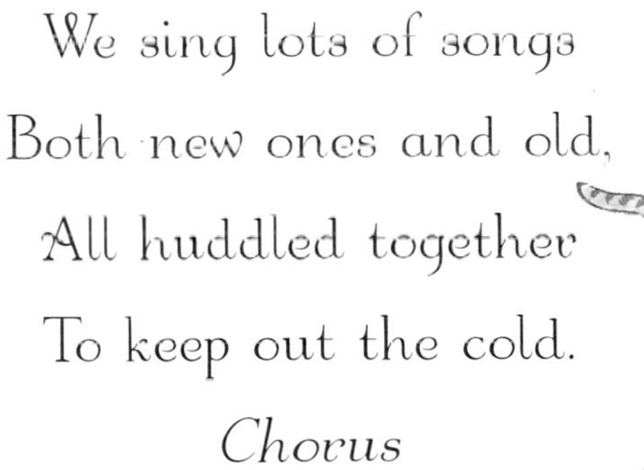

We sing lots of songs
Both new ones and old,
All huddled together
To keep out the cold.
Chorus

LAZY LION

Lazy Lion lay snoozing in the shade of a tree, flicking at the buzzing flies with his tail.

He liked nothing more than sleeping. In fact he would sleep all night and all day if he could, just waking up every once in a while to have a snack.

"Hmm," he purred to himself. "This is the life. Nothing to do all day but lie in the sun and sleep. Perfect!"

Just then, a laughing hyena ran by.

"Wake up, Lazy Lion!" he chuckled. "Or do you want a swim!? Rain's coming!"

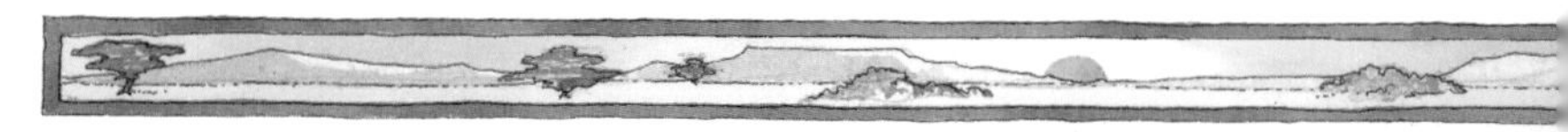

Lazy Lion opened one eye. "Silly creature!" he said, as he watched the hyena running into the distance, still laughing. "He's trying to trick me into waking up and moving!" and he closed his eyes and went back to sleep.

A short while later someone nudged his behind.

"Wake up, Lazy Lion. There's rain coming." Giraffe was bending her long neck down and nudging him with her nose. "You should head for shelter. The river might flood!"

"Don't be ridiculous!" said Lion. "I see Hyena's been filling your head with his nonsense!" and he closed his eyes and was snoring again in seconds.

But he had not been dozing for long when he felt something tugging at his whiskers.

"Wake up, Lazy Lion!" It was a little mouse. "Rain's coming. Could you please carry my children and I to safety?" asked the mouse.

"Oh, I'm far too busy for that," said Lazy Lion. "Why talk of rain? It's a fine, sunny day!" And closing his eyes he went to sleep.

A few moments later he was woken by something pulling at his tail. It was Monkey.

"Wake up, Lazy Lion. Rain's coming. Could you help carry my bananas up to the rocks?"

"Don't wake me up" said Lazy Lion, crossly. "Can't you see I'm busy?"

"But you didn't look busy," said Monkey.

"Well, I am!" growled Lion. "I'm very busy thinking what to do with the next person who wakes me up!" And he gave Monkey a mean stare, before shutting his eyes tight.

After that, none of the animals dared to wake Lazy Lion up again. So they couldn't warn him that the dark storm clouds were gathering, and the first drops of rain had started to fall.

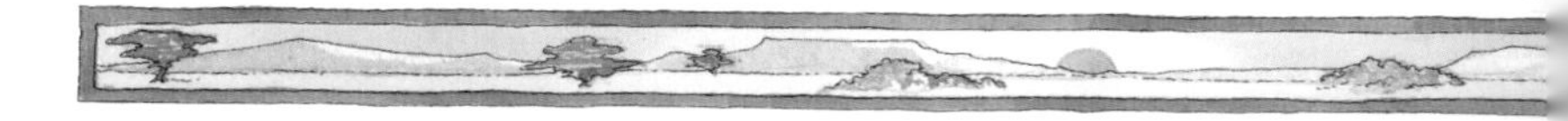

They just hurried high up to the safety of the rocks and caves and took shelter from the storm that was on its way.

Lazy Lion lay dreaming. A big raindrop fell on his nose. Then another, and another. Lion stirred. "Oh, bother," he thought to himself. "It's raining. Well, it's probably only a light shower. I'll snooze a little longer." He settled back down to sleep.

The rain began to fall harder. Soon Lazy Lion's thick fur was wet through and he began to feel cold and uncomfortable. But he was still too lazy to get up and move to the shelter of the rocks. "I'll just sleep for five more minutes!" he told himself.

The rain fell harder and harder, and the river rose higher and higher. Then, with a flash of lightening and a huge crash of thunder, the river broke its banks and came flooding across the plains! Suddenly, Lazy Lion was being tossed around as he struggled to keep his head above the stormy waters.

The other animals watched in horror from the rocks as Lazy Lion was dragged below the water by the strong current.

Then suddenly his big strong head popped up again, and he gasped for breath.

Lazy Lion swam with all his might towards the rocks, to the cheers of the animals.

"Oh, this is hard work!" he panted. How he wished he had listened to the others and had not been so lazy.

At last he made it. The other animals gathered round, anxiously.

"Oh dear, are you all right, Lazy Lion?" asked Monkey.

"I'm exhausted!" panted Lazy Lion, "but it's nothing a good sleep won't cure!"

BEARS AHOY

One summer's day, three little boys went for a picnic by the bank of a river. They took their swimming things, some sandwiches and, of course, their teddy bears.

When they arrived, they found a small boat tied to a tree. The boys climbed on board with their teddies, and had a great game of pirates. The boys pretended to walk the plank, and soon they were all splashing about in the river. They chased each other through the shallow water, and disappeared along the river and out of sight.

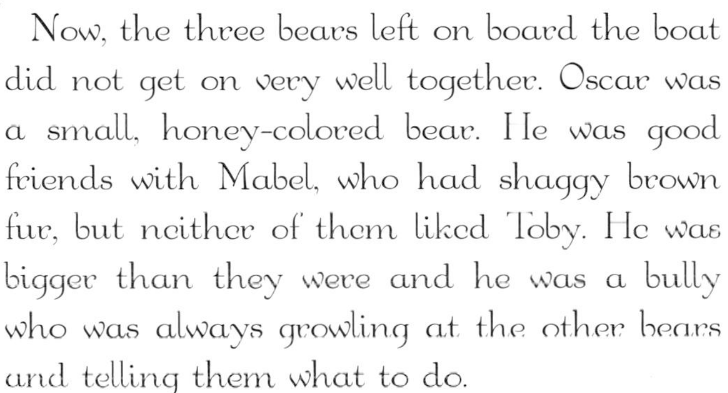

Now, the three bears left on board the boat did not get on very well together. Oscar was a small, honey-colored bear. He was good friends with Mabel, who had shaggy brown fur, but neither of them liked Toby. He was bigger than they were and he was a bully who was always growling at the other bears and telling them what to do.

As soon as the boys were out of sight, Toby leapt to his feet. The boat rocked. Oscar and Mabel begged him to sit down.

"I'm a fearless sailor," cried Toby. "I've sailed the seven seas and I'm going to sail again." He untied the boat, and pushed it away from the bank. The boat lurched from side to side.

"Look lively!" shouted Toby. "Do as I say or I'll make you walk the plank." Now that it was untied, the little blue boat began to drift. It turned sideways gently, then caught the main current and began to gather speed.

"Toby!" cried Oscar. "We're moving!"

"You big softie," growled Toby. "We're bold and fearless pirates on the high seas."

Oscar and Mabel clung together in fright, as the little boat sailed down the river, past fields and houses. "Help!" they shouted. "Make it stop!" But Toby was having a great time.

"Ha, ha," shouted Toby. "This is the life!"

Oscar glanced over the side. He wished he hadn't. The sight of everything passing by so quickly made him feel seasick.

"Look out, Toby!" he cried. "We're going to hit the bank. Steer it away."

But Toby didn't and the boat hit the bank with a thump. Toby fell forward as the boat swung round towards the middle of the river.

"Toby!" shouted Mabel. "Save us!"

But Toby was sitting in the bottom of the boat, rubbing a big bump on his head.

"I can't. I don't know how to sail a boat," he whimpered. He hid his face in his paws and began to cry. The boat zig zagged on down the river, with the little bears clinging on to the sides in fright. In time, the river became wider and they could hear the cry of seagulls.

"Oh, Toby," cried Mabel. "We're heading for the sea. Do something!"

"Nobody likes me," wailed Toby. "We're going to sink to the bottom of the sea, and you won't like me either!"

Oscar had found a rope hanging from the sail. "Let's put up the sail and see if it will blow us to shore," he said.

"We'll be blown out to sea," wailed Toby, but Oscar ignored him. The wind filled the sail and the little boat started moving forward. They sailed right across the bay to the far side, and blew up on to the beach.

"Oh, Oscar, you are a hero!" sighed Mabel, hugging him tight. "You saved us!"

Imagine the bears' surprise to see the three little boys running towards them along the beach – they were on their way to find the coastguard to raise the alarm. There were hugs and kisses all round when they found the bears safe and sound. And you from that day on, Toby was a much wiser and kinder bear, and he never bullied the others again.

The Wheels on the Bus

The wheels on the bus go round and round,
Round and round, round and round,
The wheels on the bus
go round and round,
All day long.

The wipers on
the bus go swish,
swish, swish, etc.

The horn on the bus
goes beep! beep! beep! etc.

The people on the bus go chat, chat, chat, etc.

The children on the bus bump up and down, etc.

The babies on the bus go "WAAH! WAAH! WAAH!", etc.

The grannies on the bus go knit, knit, knit, etc.

The wheels on the bus go round and round,
All day long.

Baa Baa Black Sheep

Baa, baa, black sheep,
Have you any wool?
Yes, sir, yes, sir,
Three bags full;
One for the master,
And one for the dame,
And one for the little boy
Who lives down the lane.

Hot Cross Buns!

Hot cross buns!

Hot cross buns!

One a-penny, two a-penny,

Hot cross buns!

If you have no daughters,

Give them to your sons,

One a-penny, two a-penny,

Hot cross buns!

ITCHY SPOTS

Poor Monkey was wriggling
And jiggling around,
Scratching and making
A chattering
sound:

"They're driving me mad,
Someone help me please –
I have to get rid of
These terrible fleas!"

Then along came a bear
In a bit of a stew –
"I've got such a bad itch,
I don't know what to do!

It's right in a spot
I can't reach with my paws.
So why not scratch my back,
And I will scratch yours!"

THREE TEDS IN A TUB

Rub-a-dub, dub,
Three teds in a tub,
Sailing across the sea!
But the rumble of tums,
And the smell of hot buns,
Will bring them back
home for tea!

CROCODILE SMILES

"Say cheese!" said the photographer.

"CHEESE!" grinned Snappy, the crocodile as he gave his most winning smile.

"You're a natural!" cried the expedition leader, who was with a team of wildlife photographers. Snappy smiled down at his reflection in the river.

"Ooh, what a handsome chap!" he preened, gnashing his fine set of teeth with glee.

Snappy was terribly proud of his sharp fangs, and fine good looks. He strutted up and down the river bank for all to see.

"I'm a star!" he said. "My face will be known throughout the world!"

"Thanks for letting us take your picture," said the expedition leader.

"No problem," said Snappy. "Anytime!"

"And as your reward, here's the truckload of chocolate you asked for," said the leader.

"How delicious!" said Snappy. "Most kind of you. Thank you so much."

When they had gone, Snappy lay in the sun, daydreaming of fame and fortune, and popping chocolates into his big, open mouth.

Just then, along slithered Snake.

"What's thissss?" he hissed. "A crocodile eating chocolate? How sssstrange!"

"Not at all!" snapped Snappy. "All crocodiles love chocolate. It's just that most of them don't know how to get hold of it."

"Well, if you're so sssmart, you ssshould know that too much chocolate will make your teeth fall out!" hissed Snake.

"What rot!" said Snappy, crossly. "For your information, I've got perfect teeth."

"Lucky you!" said Snake, and slithered off into the bushes.

So Snappy carried on eating chocolate. He had chocolate for breakfast, chocolate for lunch and chocolate for dinner.

"Ooh, yummy!" he grinned, smiling a big, chocolatey smile. "This is heaven."

"You won't be saying that when you are too fat to float in the river," said Parrot, who had been watching him from a tree.

"Nonsense!" scoffed Snappy. "I've got a very fine figure, I'll have you know!"

"If you say so," said Parrot, and flew off into the jungle.

Days and weeks passed with Snappy eating chocolate after chocolate, until it was all gone.

"Back to the river to catch my next meal, then," Snappy thought miserably. "Though I'd much rather have more chocolate!"

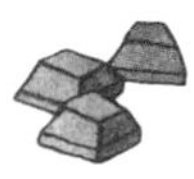

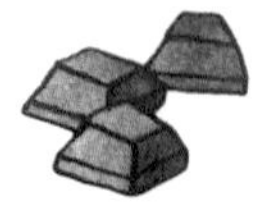

When Snappy slid into the river, instead of bobbing along gently, he sank straight to the bottom, and his stomach rested in the mud.

"Oh, dear, what's happened to the river?" Snappy wondered aloud to himself. "It's very hard to float in today."

"Even for someone with such a fine figure as you?" jeered Parrot, watching from the trees. Snappy just sank further beneath the water so that only his two beady eyes could be seen, and gave Parrot a very hard stare.

He awoke next morning with a terrible pain in his mouth. It felt as if someone was twisting his teeth. "Oww, my teeth!" he cried.

"Sssurely not!" hissed Snake, dangling down from a tree. "After all, you have sssuch perfect teeth!"

Snappy knew what he had to do. He set off down the river to visit Mr Drill the dentist.

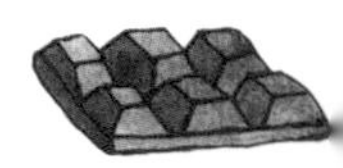

It was a long hard walk, and by the time he got there he was puffing and panting.

"Open wide!" said Mr Drill, an anteater, peering into Snappy's gaping mouth. "Oh, dear, what have you been eating, Snappy? Now show me where it hurts."

"Here," said Snappy pointing miserably into his mouth, and feeling rather ashamed, "and here, and here, and here..."

"Well, there's nothing for it," said Mr Drill, "they'll have to come out!" And so they did!

Before very long, another photography expedition arrived in the jungle.

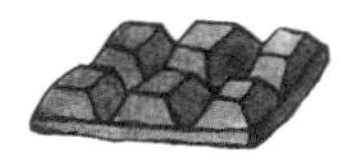

"Say cheese!" said the expedition leader.

"CHEESE!" smiled Snappy, stepping out from behind a tree. But instead of a flash of cameras, Snappy met with howls of laughter.

"I thought you told us Snappy was a handsome crocodile with perfect teeth!" they cried, looking at the leader. "He should be called Guppy, not Snappy!"

Poor Snappy slunk away into the bushes and cried. It was all his own fault for being so greedy and eating all that chocolate.

"There, there," said Mr Drill, "we'll soon fit you out with some fine new teeth."

And from then on, Snappy vowed he would never eat chocolate again!

THE BEAR WILL HAVE TO GO

While Lucy slept in the shade of a tree, Cuthbert went for a walk into the woods and was soon quite lost. So he sat down and thought about what to do next.

When Lucy awoke, she looked around in surprise. Her teddy bear, Cuthbert, was missing. She didn't know that when people are asleep their teddy bears like to go walking.

"Cuthbert!" she called. "where are you?"

He wasn't very far away. Lucy soon found him sniffing at a clump of moss.

"There you are!" she sighed. "I thought I'd lost you. Where's your vest?"

In fact, Lucy really had lost Cuthbert. The bear she was taking home was not a teddy bear at all, but a real baby bear cub! The bear in Lucy's arms kept very still, stared straight ahead, and tried not to sneeze. When they reached Lucy's bedroom she flung the bear on her bed, then went to run a bath.

"Time to escape!" thought the bear. He slid off the bed, pulling the covers after him and tried to climb up the curtains. They tumbled down into a heap on the floor. Just then Lucy's mother came into the room. The bear froze. Then Lucy appeared.

"You've been playing with that bear again, look at the mess," said Lucy's mother.

Lucy had no idea how her room had got in such a mess. She tidied up, went into the bathroom and put the bear on the edge of the tub.

"Don't fall in," she said, and went to fetch a towel. The bear jumped into the tub and then waved his paws wildly sending sprays of soapy water across the room. When he heard footsteps, he froze and floated on his back in the water as if nothing was wrong.

It was Lucy, followed by her mother. "Oh, Lucy! What a mess!"

"Cuthbert must have fallen in," cried Lucy, rubbing his wet fur with a towel.

"A teddy bear couldn't make this mess on its own," said Lucy's mother. "Please clean it up."

Lucy looked carefully at the bear. Something was different, but she couldn't work out what.

That night, while Lucy slept, the bear tip-toed downstairs. He needed to get back to the woods where he belonged, but he was hungry.

When Lucy came down for a glass of milk she found him with food all over his paws. The bear froze. Then her mother appeared in the doorway.

"This is the last straw, Lucy," said her mother, crossly. "You have been very naughty today, and every time something happens you've got that bear with you. If there is any more bad behaviour, the bear will have to go."

When her mother had gone back upstairs, Lucy looked carefully at the bear.

"You're not Cuthbert are you?" she said. The bear looked back at her and blinked. Lucy gasped. "You're a real bear!"

Now it all made sense! Lucy could hardly believe she had made such a mistake. She stroked the bear and he licked her finger.

"I'd better get you back to the woods before there's any more trouble," she said. "And I'd better try to find the real Cuthbert."

So early next morning, before her parents were awake, she crept out of the house carrying the bear. In the woods she put the bear on the ground. He licked her hand and padded away.

Lucy was sad to see the little bear go. As she wiped a tear from her eye she turned round... and there sat her teddy bear, Cuthbert! Lucy picked him up and hugged him.

"Where have you been?" she asked. "You'll never guess the trouble I've been in. What have you been doing all night?"

Cuthbert said nothing. He just smiled. What had he been doing all night? Well, that's another story!

One Finger, One Thumb

One finger, one thumb, keep moving,
One finger, one thumb, keep moving,
One finger, one thumb, keep moving,
We'll all be merry and bright.

One finger, one thumb,
one arm, keep moving,
One finger, one thumb,
one arm, keep moving,
One finger, one thumb,
one arm, keep moving,
We'll all be merry and bright.

One finger, one thumb,
one arm, one leg,
keep moving, etc

One finger, one thumb,
one arm, one leg, one nod
of the head, keep moving, etc.

Here We Go Round the Mulberry Bush

Here we go round the mulberry bush,
mulberry bush, mulberry bush,
Here we go round the mulberry bush,
on a cold and frosty morning.

This is the way we brush our hair,
brush our hair, brush our hair,
This is the way we brush our hair,
on a cold and frosty morning.

Repeat chorus

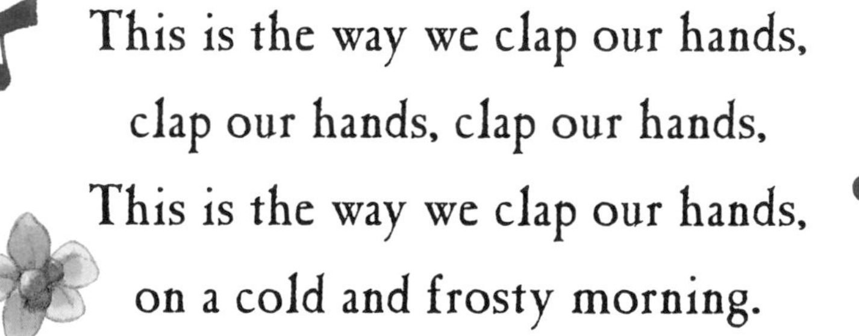

This is the way we clap our hands,
clap our hands, clap our hands,
This is the way we clap our hands,
on a cold and frosty morning.

Repeat chorus

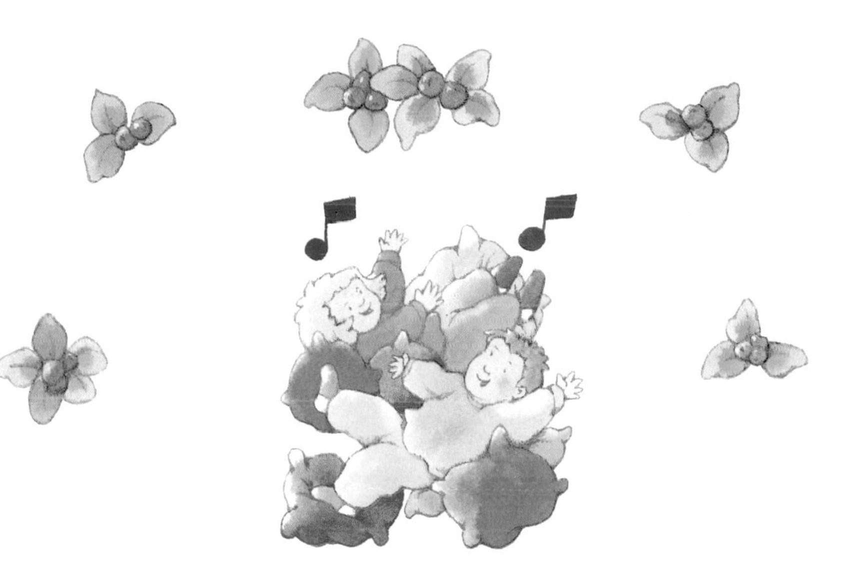

This is the way we fall on the floor,
fall on the floor, fall on the floor,
This is the way we fall on the floor,
on a cold and frosty morning.

Repeat chorus

I Love Little Pussy

I love little pussy,
her coat is so warm,
And if I don't hurt her
she'll do me no harm.

So I'll not pull her tail,
nor drive her away,
But Pussy and I very
gently will play.

Goosey, Goosey Gander

Goosey, goosey, gander,
Whither shall I wander?
Upstairs and downstairs,
And in my lady's chamber.
There I met an old man
Who would not say his prayers.
I took him by the left leg
And threw him down the stairs.

MIDNIGHT FUN

Just as midnight's striking,
When everyone's asleep,
Teddies yawn and stretch and shake,
And out of warm beds creep.

They sneak out from their houses,
And gather in the dark,
Then skip along the empty streets,
Heading for the park.

And there beneath the moonlight,
They tumble down the slides,
They swoosh up high upon the swings,
And play on all the rides.

And when the sun comes peeping,
They rush home to their beds,
And snuggle down as children wake,
To cuddle with their teds!

THE LITTLEST PIG

Little Pig had a secret. He snuggled down in the warm hay with his brothers and sisters, looked up at the dark sky twinkling with stars, and smiled a secret smile to himself. Maybe it wasn't so bad being the littlest pig after all...

Not so long ago, Little Pig had been feeling quite fed up. He was the youngest and the smallest pig in the family. He had five brothers and five sisters who were all much bigger and fatter than him. The farmer's wife called him Runt, as he was the smallest pig of the litter.

"I don't suppose little Runt will come to much," she told her friend Daisy, as they stopped by to bring the piglets some fresh hay.

His brothers and sisters teased him terribly. "Poor little Runtie," they said to him, giggling. "You must be the smallest pig in the world!"

"Leave me alone!" said Little Pig, and he crept off to the corner of the pig pen, where he curled into a ball, and started to cry. "If you weren't all so greedy, and let me have some food, maybe I'd be bigger!" he mumbled, sadly.

Every feeding time was the same – the others all pushed and shoved, and shunted Little Pig out of the way, until all that was left were the scraps. He would never grow bigger at this rate.

Then one day Little Pig made an important discovery. He was hiding in the corner of the pen, as usual, when he spied a little hole in the fence tucked away behind the feeding trough.

"I could fit through there!" thought Little Pig.

He waited all day until it was time for bed, and then, when he was sure that all of his brothers and sisters were fast asleep, he wriggled through the hole. Suddenly he was outside, free to go wherever he pleased. And what an adventure he had!

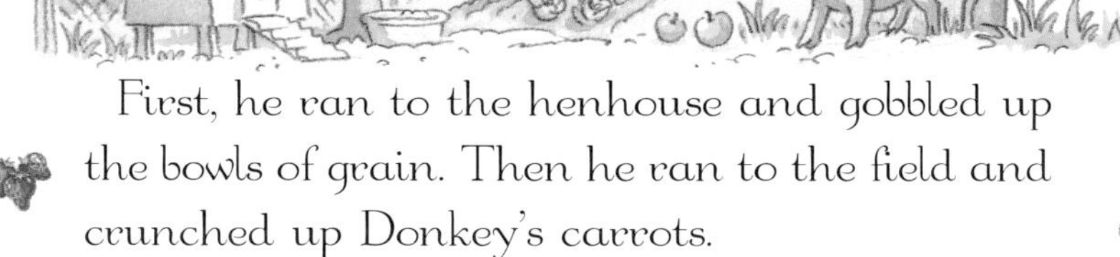

First, he ran to the henhouse and gobbled up the bowls of grain. Then he ran to the field and crunched up Donkey's carrots.

He ran to the vegetable patch and munched a row of cabbages. What a wonderful feast! Then, when he was full to bursting, he headed for home. On the way he stopped by the hedgerow. What was that lovely smell? He rooted around and found where it was coming from – a bank of wild strawberries.

Little Pig had never tasted anything so delicious. "Tomorrow night, I'll start with these!" he promised himself as he trotted back home to the pig pen.

He wriggled back through the hole, and fell fast asleep snuggled up to his mother, smiling very contentedly.

Every night Little Pig continued his tasty adventures. He didn't mind when they pushed him out of the way at feeding time, he knew that a much better feast awaited him outside. Sometimes he would find the dog's bowl filled with scraps from the farmer's supper, or buckets of oats ready for the horses. "Yum, yum – piggy porridge!" he would giggle, and gobbled it up.

But as the days and weeks went by, and Little Pig grew bigger and fatter, it was more of a squeeze to wriggle through the hole each night.

Little Pig knew that soon he wouldn't be able to fit through the hole, but by then he would be big enough to stand up to his brothers and sisters. And for now he was enjoying his secret!

BARNEY THE BOASTFUL BEAR

Barney was a very boastful bear.

"Look at my lovely soft fur!" he would say to the other toys. "See how it shines!"

Barney loved to talk about himself. "I'm the smartest toy in the playroom!" he would say. He didn't know that the other toys all laughed about him behind his back.

"That bear thinks he's so smart," growled Scotty Dog. "But he isn't smart enough to know when everyone's fed up with him!"

"He'll learn his lesson one of these days," said Molly Monkey, and sure enough, that is just what happened...

One summer's day, the toys lazed in the warm playroom. "Wouldn't it be lovely if we could go for a walk outside," said Rag Doll.

"Even better, we could go for a drive in the toy car!" said Rabbit.

"But none of us is big or clever enough to drive the toy car," said Rag Doll, sadly.

"I am!" came a voice from the corner. It was Barney. He had been sitting quietly, listening to all the toys talking.

"I can drive the toy car, and I know a place for a picnic," he said.

"We've never seen you drive the car," said Rabbit, suspiciously.

"That's because I drive it at night, when you're asleep," said Barney. "I'm a very good driver, in fact."

"Ooh, let's go then!" cried Rag Doll. In no time they had packed up a picnic and were sitting ready in the car.

"Er, I don't feel like driving today, actually," mumbled Barney. "It's too hot."

But the others weren't interested in hearing excuses, so Barney reluctantly climbed into the driver's seat and started the engine. The truth was, Barney had never really driven the car before, but he wanted to show off, so he pretended to know what he was doing.

Off they set down the garden path. "Toot, toot!" Barney beeped the horn as he turned the car out into the country lane, and soon they were driving along, singing merrily.

All was going well, until Rag Doll suddenly said, "Hey, Barney, didn't we just miss the turning for the woods?"

"I know where I'm going," said Barney, crossly. "Leave it to me," and he made the little car go faster.

"Slow down a bit, Barney!" called Old Bear, from the back seat. "My fur is getting all ruffled." He was starting to feel anxious.

"I don't need a back seat driver," said Barney, with a growl, and made the car go even faster. The others were feeling scared, but Barney was having a great time.

"I'm a wonderful driver!" he chuckled. "Look – no hands!" And he took his paws off the steering wheel. Just then they reached a sharp corner. The little car went spinning off the side of the road and crashed into a tree, tipping all the toys out into the ditch!

Luckily no one was hurt. They were not pleased with Barney though.

"You're a silly bear!" said Rabbit, crossly. "We could have all been badly hurt!"

"We'll have to walk home now," said Rag Doll, rubbing her head. "Where are we?"

Everyone looked at Barney.

"Don't ask me!" he said, quietly.

"But you said you knew the way!" said Old Bear, indignantly.

"I was only pretending," said Barney, his voice trembling. "I don't really know how to drive, and I don't know where we are!" Then he started to cry.

The other toys were furious with Barney.

"You naughty boastful bear!" they scolded. "See what trouble your boasting has caused!"

The lost toys walked through the dark woods all night long, clinging together in fright as shadows loomed around them.

They had never been out at night before. Just before dawn, they spotted their little house, and crept back into the playroom.

Luckily their owner had not noticed they were missing, so she never knew what an adventure her toys had while she was asleep, but she often wondered what had happened to her toy car.

As for Barney, he was very sorry for the trouble he had caused. The other toys forgave him, and from that day on he never boasted about anything again.

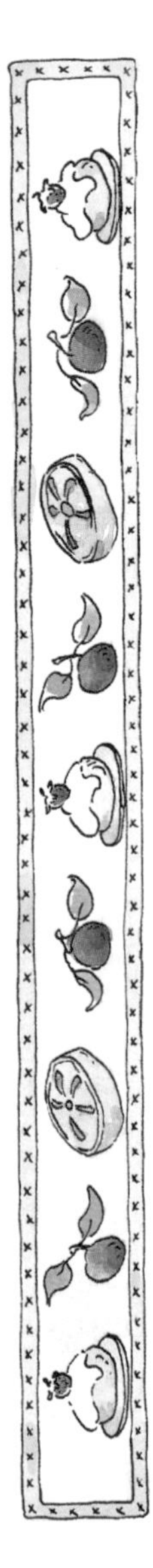

THE END

Illustrations by:
Georgie Birkett, Stephanie Boey, Mario Capaldi, Dorothy Clark, Kate Davies, Maggie Downer, Frank Endersby, Serena Feneziani, Andrew Geeson, Piers Harper, Elaine Keary, Claire Mumford, Rikki O'Neill, Pauline Siewart, Jessica Stockham, Linda Worrell.

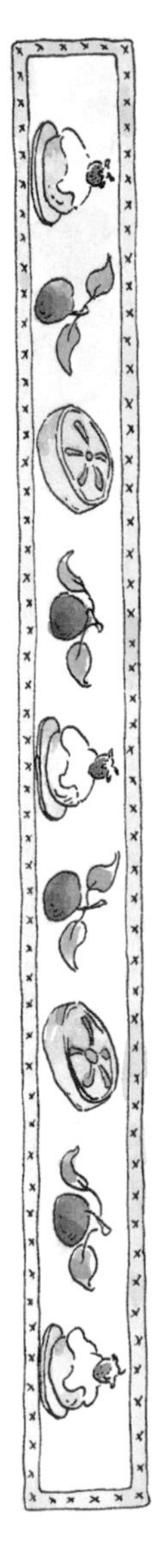